BLUE HEN
and
Her Babies

ISBN: 978-1-950791-00-2

Cover and text layout design: Kristi Yoder

Artist: Eva Zimmerman

Printed in China

Published by:

TGS International
P.O. Box 355
Berlin, Ohio 44610 USA
Phone: 330.893.4828
Fax: 330.893.2305
www.tgsinternational.com

TGS0001967

BLUE HEN
and
Her Babies

Eva Zimmerman

Introduction

Blue Hen was a Lavender Orpington hen who wanted to be a mother hen. Her story is based on true happenings. Blue Hen lived at a hatchery, where many kinds of babies were always ready to be mothered. The baby chicks Blue Hen raised were for the next year's chicken flock. Blue Hen was careful not to lose any of them. I hope you will enjoy hearing about Blue Hen and her babies.

–Eva Zimmerman

Blue Hen was a big, beautiful hen with shiny, blue-gray feathers. Every day Blue Hen darted around the green meadow with the other hens. Every day she raced to catch the biggest, juiciest bugs. Every day she went to the little creek for a drink of cool water.

And every day Blue Hen went into the hen house and laid one brown egg on the nest of straw.

But Blue Hen wanted to be a mother hen. She stopped going to the meadow with the other hens. She stopped racing for the biggest bugs and going for a drink at the creek. She stopped laying her egg every day. She just sat in the hen house on a nest—any nest that held an egg—all day and all night.

Finally someone gave Blue Hen some
duck eggs. And Blue Hen sat and sat
on those duck eggs. At last, one day,
seven fluffy baby ducks hatched out.
Oh, Blue Hen was happy!
Now she was a mother hen!

Blue Hen clucked and clucked to her babies. She led them out to the green meadow. She showed them how to find the biggest bugs. She led them to the little creek to get a drink. She warmed them under her blue-gray feathers when they got cold. Blue Hen was a good mother hen.

But baby ducks are ducks after all, and when Blue Hen took them to the little creek, they happily splashed right into the water. When it rained, into the puddles those seven babies went. Poor Blue Hen! She did not like to get her feet wet! But she wanted to be with her babies, so into the puddles she went with her seven baby ducks! She was a good mother hen.

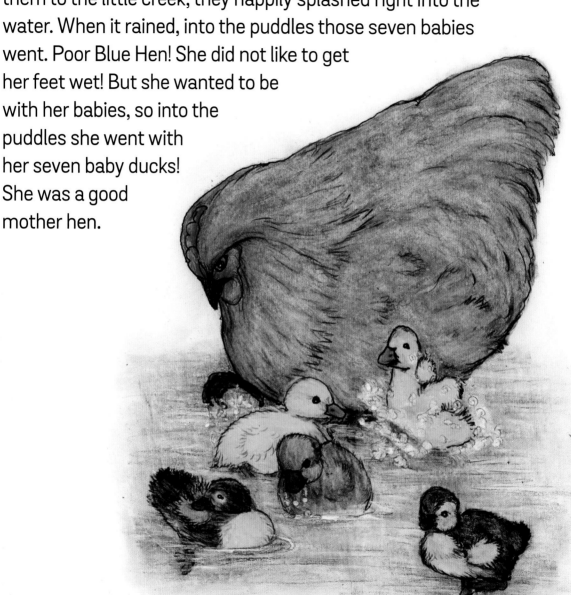

Baby ducks grow fast—very fast! It was not
long at all until they found the big creek. Out into
the water they swam. Out into the deep water
of the big creek. Oh, how they liked to swim!

But here Blue Hen could not follow. She could not swim, no matter how much she wanted to be with her babies. There she sat, on the banks of the big creek, waiting and waiting. When her babies came out of the water, they snuggled right under her fine blue-gray feathers.

The baby ducks grew and grew. Soon the time came when they did not need Blue Hen at all anymore. Not even her warm, fluffy feathers.

Blue Hen still wanted to be a mother
hen. So back on her nest she sat.
Then someone gave her five baby
guineas. Oh, Blue Hen was happy!
She had babies again!

16

Out into the green meadow Blue Hen led her baby guineas. Out to the little stream to get a cool drink. The baby guineas did not splash right into the water as the ducks did. They stayed close by her and chased after bugs in the warm sunshine day after happy day.

Baby guineas grow feathers and soon learn to fly. It was not long at all until those baby guineas flew high, high up into a tree. That is where they wanted to sleep, and that is where they stayed all night. Blue Hen wanted her babies, but she could not fly. She clucked and clucked. But baby guineas are guineas after all, and they would not come down.

When morning came, the baby guineas flew down and stayed close by Blue Hen all day. They chased bugs with her. The guineas grew and grew. Soon the time came when they did not need Blue Hen at all anymore. Not even to chase bugs.

Blue Hen was sad. She wanted to be a mother hen. So back on her nest she sat. And someone gave her more babies. Not five babies, not seven babies, but forty babies! Not duck babies, not guinea babies, but chicken babies. Forty baby chicks!

Oh, Blue Hen was happy! How busy she was! She led her babies out to the green meadow to catch bugs. She took them to the little creek to get a drink. She warmed them under her feathers. Babies, babies, babies everywhere! These babies did not swim in the creek. They did not fly high, high up in the trees. They just scratched in the dirt like Blue Hen did. They did everything just like Blue Hen did.

Blue Hen scratched a hole in the soft dust. Now all her baby chicks could fit underneath her shiny blue-gray feathers. She led them to the places where someone had scattered feed for them. She clucked and clucked to call them into a warm box at night. She was a good mother hen—very good. She did not lose any of her forty babies, not even one. Blue Hen and her forty baby chicks played outside in the bright sunshine day after happy day, all summer long.

Blue Hen loved babies.
Duck babies, guinea babies, chick babies.
Brown babies, yellow babies, spotted babies.
Blue Hen wanted them all.

God loves children.
Brown children, white children, black children.
Chinese children, Indian children, all children.
BIG children, little children.
Young children, old children.
God wants them all.

Jesus calls His children to Him and keeps them safe, just like the mother hen clucks to her babies and gathers them under her wings!

"... How often would I have
gathered thy children together,
even as a hen gathers her
chickens under her wings ..."
Matthew 23:37

THE END

About the Author

Eva Zimmerman lives in Lancaster County, Pennsylvania, where she taught special education for 25 years. She enjoyed reading picture books to her students.

She has enjoyed the animals that have lived at her home over the years. Their antics and unique traits have provided her with many stories to tell.

Her hobbies include bird watching, nature walks, drawing, painting, and carving. She also enjoys entertaining children.

Eva desires to use her talents to the honor and glory of God. You can contact Eva by writing to her in care of Christian Aid Ministries, P. O. Box 360, Berlin, OH 44610.

About Christian Aid Ministries

Christian Aid Ministries was founded in 1981 as a nonprofit, tax-exempt 501(c)(3) organization. Its primary purpose is to provide a trustworthy and efficient channel for Amish, Mennonite, and other conservative Anabaptist groups and individuals to minister to physical and spiritual needs around the world. This is in response to the command to ". . . do good unto all men, especially unto them who are of the household of faith" (Galatians 6:10).

Each year, CAM supporters provide 15–20 million pounds of food, clothing, medicines, seeds, Bibles, Bible story books, and other Christian literature for needy people. Most of the aid goes to orphans and Christian families. Supporters' funds also help to clean up and rebuild for natural disaster victims, put up Gospel billboards in the U.S., support several church-planting efforts, operate two medical clinics, and provide resources for needy families to make their own living. CAM's main purposes for providing aid are to help and encourage God's people and bring the Gospel to a lost and dying world.

CAM has staff, warehouses, and distribution networks in Romania, Moldova, Ukraine, Haiti, Nicaragua, Liberia, Israel, and Kenya. Aside from management, supervisory personnel, and bookkeeping operations, volunteers do most of the work at CAM locations. Each year, volunteers at our warehouses, field bases, Disaster Response Services projects, and other locations donate over 200,000 hours of work.

CAM's ultimate purpose is to glorify God and help enlarge His kingdom. ". . . whatsoever ye do, do all to the glory of God" (1 Corinthians 10:31).